Rookie reader

SHOW-AND-TELL SAM

BY
CHARNAN
SIMON

ILLUSTRATED
BY
GARY BIALKE

SCHOLASTIC INC.
New York   Toronto   London   Auckland   Sydney
Mexico City   New Delhi   Hong Kong   Buenos Aires

For Millie, Maude, and Riley,
who all know how to behave in school.
—C. S.

For Ms. Shlobotnik, who always said I'd excel in "Nap Time."
—G. B.

Reading Consultant
Linda Cornwell
Learning Resource Consultant
Indiana Department of Education

ISBN 0-516-24142-7

Text copyright © 1998 by Charnan Simon. Illustrations copyright © 1998 by Gary Bialke. All rights reserved. Published by Scholastic Inc., 557 Broadway, New York, NY 10012. SCHOLASTIC and associated logos are trademarks and/or registered trademarks of Scholastic Inc.

12 11 10 9 8 7 6   3 4 5 6 7/0

Printed in the U.S.A.   10

First Scholastic printing, May 2002

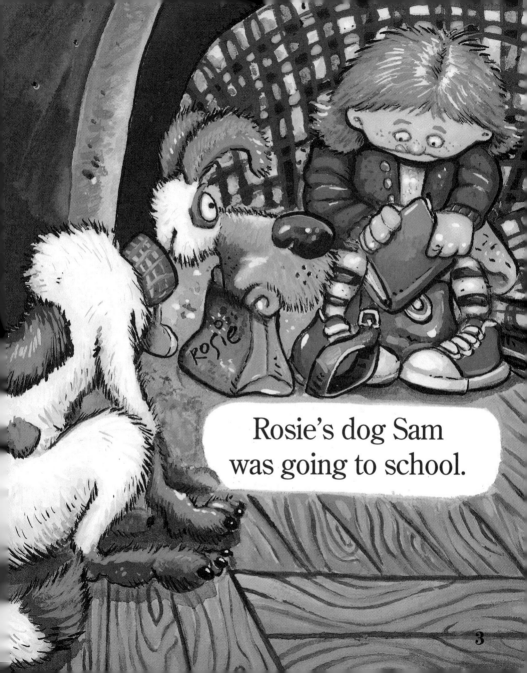

Rosie's dog Sam
was going to school.

3

"You can be my show-and-tell,"
Rosie said.

Sam could hardly wait.

He showed Rosie
a shortcut to school,

and how to line up at the door.

10

12

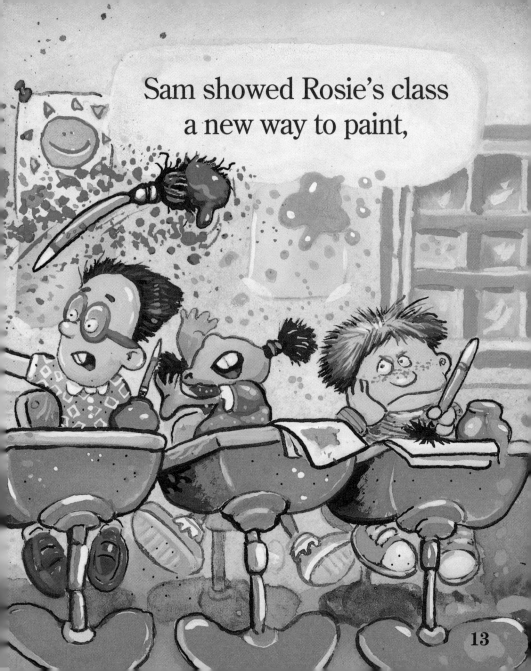

Sam showed Rosie's class
a new way to paint,

14

He showed them how
much he liked Teacher,

16

and tadpoles,

21

and best of all—snack time!

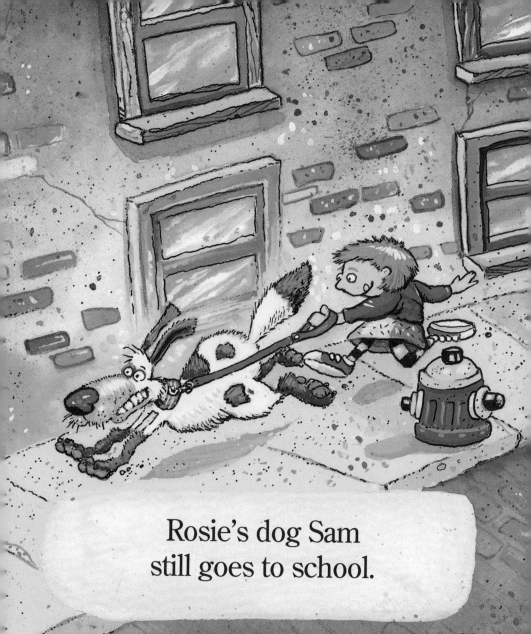

Rosie's dog Sam
still goes to school.

He misses snack time.

WORD LIST (53 words)

a	hardly	pencils	tell
all	he	Rosie's	the
and	him	said	them
at	home	Sam	time
be	how	school	to
best	it	sharpen	too
can	liked	shortcut	up
class	line	show-and-tell	wait
could	misses	showed	was
dog	much	singing	way
door	my	snack	you
go	new	still	
goes	of	tadpoles	
going	paint	Teacher	

ABOUT THE AUTHOR

Charnan Simon lives is Madison, Wisconsin, with her husband, Tom Kazunas, and her daughters, Ariel and Hana. Charnan spends her time reading and writing books and keeping up with her very busy family. Other Rookie Readers by Charnan Simon include *Sam and Dasher* and *Come! Sit! Speak!*

ABOUT THE ILLUSTRATOR

Gary Bialke lives in the upper left-hand corner of the United States with five shedding machines. He barks at strangers and sleeps twenty hours a day. It's only his long hind legs and opposable thumbs that make him the pack leader. He is loved by veterinarians everywhere.